for
Jo
someone very special

How the Trollusk Got His Hat

by Mercer Mayer

gb Golden Press • New York

Western Publishing Company, Inc.
Racine, Wisconsin

ne day Reggie McLeod set off for a walk to town. He wore his new Squeezle skin hat and was feeling very dapper indeed.

Quite suddenly a strong gust of wind puffed up.

It blew Reggie's new hat right off his head and carried it high into the sky.

"Stop that hat!" cried Reggie.

He rushed to the local airfield and rented a plane.
Down the runway he roared in a 1911 Fizzbat.

But, alas, the Fizzbat didn't quite make it off the ground.

There was little else for Reggie to do but go home—so that's what he did.

The wind carried Reggie's hat miles and miles across the sky to the Edge of Nowhere and blew it through an open window . . .

MY HAPPY HOME

. . . into a pot of tango soup which a Stamp-Collecting Trollusk was making for lunch.

The Trollusk noticed Reggie's name and address
stenciled inside the hat, so he set out to return it.
You see, he was an honest Trollusk.

He tried to mail the hat at the post
office but the postmaster simply shrieked
and slammed the door to his cage.

Eek!

OUT TO LUNCH
GO AWAY

LOCAL

OUT OF TOWN

AIR MAIL

OTHER

JUNK MAIL

GARBAGE

WANTED

NORA COLLITON
5½ TIN CAN ST.
YOU NAME IT CT.

Joel Beauvais
3 Bumbridge Rd.
Biddle Diddle Ct.

Cassandra Beauvais
3 Bumbridge Rd
Biddle Diddle Ct.

He tried to get on a bus but it drove away in reverse.

He tried hitchhiking but no one would stop.

He managed to buy a train ticket
but the train left without him.

He went into a local cafe to get a bite to eat but there was such a commotion that he had to leave.

Finally, he started off on foot,
to find Reggie the best way he could.

Meanwhile, Reggie appeared on national
television to ask people to look for his missing Squeezle skin hat.
Nobody paid any attention.

Poor Reggie. He went to an amusement park to cheer himself up. But even the roller coaster was no fun without his hat.

He went to museums and saw wonderful works of art.
Still he could think of nothing but his missing
Squeezle skin hat.

He tried long nature
walks in the woods.

He took up mountain climbing . . .

. . . and often went to the movies.
Finally, there was only one thing left to do.

Reggie went to the tailor's and bought a new suit and a fancy Pindofez hat. He left feeling very dapper indeed . . .

. . . and ran smack dab into the Stamp-Collecting Trollusk, who happened to be passing that way.

They introduced themselves, and the
Trollusk immediately returned the Squeezle
skin hat to Reggie.

Reggie was overjoyed and promptly gave the Trollusk the new Pindofez hat.

To celebrate the happy outcome, Reggie invited the Trollusk home for dinner.

They became fast friends and the Trollusk stayed on with Reggie for some time. During the week the Trollusk worked on his vast stamp collection. And Reggie wrote an important paper on old dinosaur bones.

WORLD'S SMALLEST STAMP

WORLD'S BIGGEST

EDGE OF NOWHERE

3d

STAMP

MY FIRST LETTER

ISLAND JOE FURNITURE CO.

ISLAND JOE FURNITURE CO.

THIS STORY IS ALMOST FINISHED. HOW DO YOU LIKE IT SO FAR?

On Sundays they went to church together and felt very dapper indeed.